**What was Indiana Jones doing
in Russia in the summer of 1913?**

Indiana Jones is that world-famous, whip-cracking hero you know from the movies....

But was he *always* cool and fearless in the face of danger? Did he *always* get mixed up in hair-raising, heart-stopping adventures?

Yes!

Read all about Indy as a kid. And meet his friend Tamara. She's a princess. Some want to see her on the throne. And others want to see her...dead!

Watch Indy come to the rescue. It's edge-of-your-seat excitement!

YOUNG INDIANA JONES™

and the
PRINCESS OF PERIL

By Les Martin

Random House New York

To Nicole, my inspiration,
who chose not to become a princess

Copyright © 1991 by Lucasfilm Ltd. (LFL)
All rights reserved under International and Pan-American Copyright
Conventions. Published in the United States by Random House, Inc.,
New York, and simultaneously in Canada by Random House of Canada
Limited, Toronto.

Young Indy novels are conceived and produced by Random House, Inc.,
in conjunction with Lucasfilm Ltd.

Library of Congress Cataloging-in-Publication Data
Martin, Les. Young Indiana Jones and the Princess of Peril / by Les Martin.
p. cm. Summary: In 1913 in Russia, Indy befriends a young Georgian
princess involved in the Georgian independence movement and is pursued by
secret police and agents of an evil religious fanatic. ISBN 0-679-81178-8 (pbk.)
— ISBN 0-679-91178-2 (lib. bdg.) [1. Soviet Union—History—1904–1914—Fiction.
2. Adventure and adventurers—Fiction.] I. Title. PZ7.M36353Y1 1991
[Fic]—dc20   90-52817

Manufactured in the United States of America   10 9 8 7 6 5 4 3 2 1

TM & © 1991 Lucasfilm Ltd. (LFL). All rights reserved.

YOUNG INDIANA JONES™
and the
PRINCESS OF PERIL

Chapter 1

Young Indiana Jones couldn't pretend that the jouncing of the train was keeping him from reading. The train ride was one of the smoothest in the world. He was aboard the Nord Express, a crack luxury train. It ran from Paris, France, to St. Petersburg, the capital of Russia.

The truth was, Indy was bored. He had been reading this book on American history for hours. American history was not Indy's favorite subject. He liked history. In fact, he loved history. But American history was so short compared to that of other countries. There simply wasn't enough of it.

He had a lot of it to read now, though. Book after book. A couple of them with him in the compartment. Others in his trunk in the baggage car. His dad had picked them out. He had decided that Indy's schoolwork had been set back by the boy's adventures around the globe. Indy had learned a lot of things, but none of them would help him pass American history.

It wasn't fair, Indy thought. He looked at his dad, seated across from him. His dad, as usual, had his nose in a history book. But not American history. Professor Henry Jones had Georgia on his mind. But instead of the state of Georgia in the American South, it was the region of Georgia in the south of Russia.

That was where they were going. St. Petersburg was their first stop. Indy's dad had to get official permission there to go on to

Georgia. He was also to meet the man putting up the money for this trip.

The man was rich and generous. That's why they were going first class. If Professor Jones were footing the bill, Indy figured, they'd be traveling by cattle car. Indy's dad did not believe in spending money on anything but books.

The stranger's offer had come out of the blue. He was a Georgian, and he wanted Georgia to take its proper place in history. He had read that Indy's dad was interested in exploits of the Crusaders in Georgia centuries ago. The man invited the professor to Georgia to find out more.

Needless to say, the professor jumped at the chance. There was one problem, though. Indy.

Indy was supposed to stay with his friend Herman while his dad was away. The night before the professor was to leave, the phone rang. It was Herman's mom. Herman had measles. That left the professor with Indy on his hands. And with just time enough to buy an extra train ticket for him to New York. And an extra ocean liner ticket to France. But there was no way to get an extra compartment on the Nord Express. The train was sold out. Indy and his dad had to share the same compartment.

Neither of them liked the arrangement. For Indy, it meant he had to keep reading American history. And for his dad, it meant the professor couldn't do as much reading as he wanted. It was hard even for Professor Jones to forget he was a father with Indy right across from him. He felt obliged to cast an occasional glance at his son. And now and then make an educational remark to him.

Right now, though, the professor had managed to forget about Indy. He was centuries away, deep in the Middle Ages. Indy could look out the window and watch forests and fields whizzing by.

There was a knock on the door. It swung open. A blue-uniformed conductor poked his head into the compartment. "Gentlemen, we change trains in twenty minutes," he announced in heavily accented English.

"I thought this train went straight through to St. Petersburg," Indy said after the conductor left.

"It does, and it doesn't," said Professor Jones. "Russia has wider railroad tracks than the rest of the world. At the border, we change to a train that runs on Russian rails. Otherwise, it's exactly like this one."

"Sounds like Russia is a real different kind of place," said Indy. He felt a spark of interest. He caught a glimmer of what he liked best in the world. The unknown.

"You'll soon see how different," Indy's dad said.

"I believe you," Indy said, looking forward to the border crossing.

Indy was right to believe his dad. Professor Jones knew what he was talking about. Russia was going to be different.

But his dad could not suspect how different Indy would find it.

And how dangerous that difference would be.

Chapter 2

Meanwhile, Professor Jones brought Indy back to the present with a dull thud.

"We have a good deal of time before we change trains," he said. "Try making progress on the book you're reading. It's the American Revolution, am I right?"

"Yeah," Indy said. "I'm stuck in Valley Forge. Going to be a long winter there."

The professor went back to his book, and Indy tried to go back to his. But the print blurred. Indy kept sneaking glances out the window. Soon the scene outside slowed. The train came to a halt, and a bell sounded.

"Saved," Indy said to himself. He and his dad left the train, carrying their hand luggage. They were on the platform of the railroad station in a small town. Indy read its sign.

"Verzhbolovo-Eydtkuhen." He sounded out the letters. "What a name!"

His dad smiled. "Read the name printed below it."

Indy looked at the weird symbols there. "What kind of writing is that?" he said.

"It's the Cyrillic alphabet," Professor Jones explained. "The alphabet used in Russia. Entirely different from ours."

"Hey, Russia is sounding more interesting all the time," Indy said. They moved toward twin checkpoints on the platform.

It was the border. Soldiers and officials of Germany under Kaiser Wilhelm II faced soldiers and officials of Russia under Czar Nicholas II. That much Indy knew from reading the papers. Squabbles between the two countries often made front-page news.

Officials of both countries glanced at Professor Jones's papers. They waved him and Indy through. Another train was waiting. It was identical to the first.

"It's a funny feeling crossing a border," Indy remarked. "On one side, they speak German. On the other, Russian. Just because of a line on a map."

"Actually, the people around here don't speak German *or* Russian," Indy's dad said. "They speak Polish."

"You mean we're in Poland?" Indy asked, puzzled.

"There is no Poland anymore," his dad explained. "It was divided among different countries over a century ago."

"I bet the Poles aren't crazy about that," Indy commented.

"They've tried to win independence," Indy's father said. "Especially from Russia, which owns most of the country. But the czar's soldiers have crushed them every time."

"So Russia doesn't have just Russians in it," Indy said.

"Not at all," said Indy's father. "Russia is an empire. It is made up of countries conquered over the centuries. Take Georgia, where we're going. They speak Georgian there. They even have their own alphabet. But Russia rules them."

"Have they tried to win independence too?" asked Indy.

"Their last uprising was put down forty years ago," said his dad. "But there's still unrest. That's why we have to get government permission to go there. The czar doesn't want to let in foreign troublemakers."

Indy's eyes lit up. Georgia sounded like a place where things were happening.

Professor Jones caught that look. Knowing Indy, he knew what it meant. His voice was stern. "That's why we must be extra-careful there. No getting mixed up in local affairs. One wrong move, and we'd be told to leave. The czar has spies everywhere. In Georgia, I want you to stick to your books. Understand?"

"I catch your meaning," sighed Indy. It was going to be a long, long visit.

At that moment, an official came up to Professor Jones. "Pardon me," he said. "I must have the key to your trunks."

"There's nothing in them but clothing and books," the professor said indignantly.

The official did not budge. "No argument. The keys. Or we break the trunks open."

Professor Jones gave him the keys and showed him the trunks. They were among many on the platform. The contents of the first train's baggage car were being shifted to the other.

"He wasn't kidding about breaking locks," said Indy. He watched soldiers smash open a large steamer trunk. They must not have located the owner. With the soldiers were two men in civilian clothes. They checked the trunk, then moved on.

"They don't kid about matters of security in Russia," said Professor Jones.

"Those two guys in civies—you think they were government spies?" asked Indy.

"It wouldn't surprise me," said his dad. "Let's get to our compartment. There's trouble in the air, and I want to steer clear of it."

"But—" said Indy as he watched the soldiers and the possible spies.

"No buts. Come on, Junior," said his dad.

"I've asked you not to call me—" Indy began.

But a conductor interrupted him.

"Good news, sir," he said to Indy's dad. "I've found a space for the boy. Somebody left a compartment vacant at the border."

In Paris, the professor had offered the man a tip if he could find an empty compartment for Indy. There had been none. But now the conductor came to claim the ten-dollar bill that the professor had flashed. The professor handed it over. The extra reading he could do would be worth it.

"Don't forget your history book," Professor Jones told Indy.

"It's right in my carrying bag," Indy assured him. He didn't mention the other book there: *Ten Bullets to Tombstone.* By Sam Magee, Indy's favorite writer of Westerns.

The conductor led him to the compartment. It had a double bunk, probably for families with kids. Still, it was luxurious. It had wooden paneling and green glass tulip-shaped lamps.

"Satisfactory?" asked the conductor.

"Great," said Indy.

The door closed. Indy grinned. Alone at last. He opened his bag and grabbed his Western. He was eager to curl up with it. He jumped into the bottom bunk and—

He stiffened. He had flopped down on something soft. Something warm. Something alive and flailing with two furious fists.

Chapter 3

"Hey, whoa," Indy said. He leapt from the bunk. Fortunately, the person in the bunk didn't pack much of a punch. Indy wasn't stunned, just startled.

He took a good look at his attacker. He got another surprise.

It was a teen-ager. A boy wearing a suit that was a little too big for him and a cap too large for his head.

The boy got a look at Indy as well.

"I am so sorry," the boy said. "I was having a bad dream when you suddenly woke me."

"No harm done," said Indy. "And I'm the one who should apologize. Sorry for barging in. The conductor said this compartment was empty. He must have made a mistake. Or else wanted a tip real bad."

"No, no," the boy said hastily. "It was I who made the mistake. I must have read my ticket wrong. I will leave now."

"Look," Indy started to propose. "Why don't we just call the conductor and—"

"No, no," the boy repeated more strongly. "I will leave now. Sorry for the bother."

Before Indy could say anything more, the boy was out the door.

Funny, Indy thought. The boy spoke perfect English, with only a slight accent. What was even stranger, he had no baggage. Indy sensed a mystery. But he couldn't see any way to pursue it. He shrugged. Too bad. He lay down in the bottom bunk and opened up *Ten Bullets to Tombstone*.

Before he even reached the first shoot-out, the door swung open. It was the boy.

"Please. Help me hide," the boy pleaded.

Indy didn't ask questions. As far as he was concerned, the world was divided: kids on one side, grownups on the other. And Indy knew which side he was on when it was showdown time.

"Quick," said Indy. "Under the blanket."

The boy did as told. Indy got in beside him, under the blanket. Indy lifted his knees in an upside-down V, so that the blanket formed a kind of tent. The bulge of the boy beside him disappeared.

There was a knock on the door.

"Come in," Indy said.

The conductor opened the door and let in two men. Indy recognized them: the two men in civies who had been going through the trunks on the platform.

The first of them barked something at Indy in Russian.

"Sorry, don't speak the language," Indy said.

"Boy. You see any strangers?" the man demanded. He spoke in harsh, heavily accented English.

"Strangers?" said Indy. "What strangers?"

"We search the compartment," the other man said in a no-nonsense voice.

Then the conductor spoke to them in Russian. They shrugged and backed off.

"You see a stranger, you must tell us. Or you be in big trouble," the first man warned before they left.

The boy came out of hiding. He sat next to Indy on the bunk.

"Lucky for me that your father is a famous professor," the boy said. "The conductor told them who he was. The secret police do not like important foreigners to see them do their dirty work. Russia wants to show a good face to its allies in the West."

"So they *were* secret police," said Indy. "And they were hunting you."

Before the boy could begin to explain, Indy went on. "Let me see if I can figure this out. It was you they were hunting for in those trunks. But you slipped out in time. And you found this compartment empty. Or maybe you had it arranged that it would be empty when the train reached the border."

The boy shook his head in wonder. "Amazing. You should be a detective."

"I'm going to be an archeologist when I grow up," Indy said. "That means doing a lot of historical detective work. I'm training myself to put together clues to find answers."

"I think you are going to be a very good archeologist," the boy said. "But, tell me, what other clues about me do you have?"

"You're not an ordinary Russian," Indy said. "You speak very good English."

"And French. And German. And Italian. And—" The boy hesitated. "And several other languages, too."

"Where did you learn them?" Indy asked.

"In Switzerland," the boy said. "I have been in school there for several years. I would still be in school there if the czar's secret police had not discovered where I was. Fortunately, they were clumsy in asking about me. I was able to get to Paris and on this train back to Russia one step ahead of them."

"So you're Russian," Indy said.

The boy started to say something. Then he hesitated again. "Yes, I am Russian, with a true Russian name. Ivan," he said. "As you may know, Russia is ruled by a czar. A bad czar. A tyrant. He imprisons or kills those who oppose his power. Yet many do. My father is one of them. He hopes for revolution. And when it comes, he wants me to be part of it. That was why he sent me abroad to get the education I needed. After the revolution, Russia will need leaders who can deal with the rest of the world."

"And he was caught?" said Indy.

Ivan nodded sadly. "A government secret agent got into his group. They put him in jail. And found out about me."

"Sounds like Russia isn't very safe for you," said Indy. "Yet you're going back."

"It is my country," the boy said. "Besides,

there are people who will give me shelter—
if I can get off this train at St. Petersburg
without the police spotting me."

"One good thing: we get into St. Petersburg
at night," Indy said. "It'll be easier to slip
away in the dark."

"You don't know St. Petersburg in summer," the boy said. "It stays light all the time.
They have what they call 'white nights.' The
darkest it gets is a couple of hours of pale
twilight in the middle of the night."

"Days without nights," Indy mused.
"Russia is strange. Tell me, do they have
those 'white nights' in Georgia, too?"

An odd look passed over Ivan's face. It
vanished as swiftly as it had appeared. "No,
just in the far north," he said in a casual
voice. "Why do you ask?"

"After St. Petersburg, my dad and I are
going down to Georgia," Indy said. "You ever
been there?"

"No, never," Ivan said. "But I've heard it's
very beautiful."

"I just hope it isn't too dull," said Indy.

"Sometimes it isn't so bad when things are dull," the boy commented dryly.

Indy grinned. "Hey, I'm sorry. Here I am worrying about my little problems when you're the one in big trouble. But don't worry. We'll get you out of this jam. I'll think of something. Trust me."

Ivan gave Indy a long look. Then he grinned. "You know," he said. "It's funny, but I do."

Chapter 4

As the train rolled toward St. Petersburg, Indy lay on the bottom bunk. *Ten Bullets to Tombstone* rested ignored on his chest. He was trying to come up with a plan. Finally he yelled up to Ivan, "I've got it."

Ivan was lying on the top bunk. He had borrowed Indy's book on the American Revolution. Indy warned him it might be boring, but Ivan shook his head. He assured Indy that nothing having to do with a revolution was boring in Russia. In fact, he was eager to read it when he glimpsed the title.

Ivan swung himself down. He and Indy sat side by side on the bottom bunk.

"You have a plan?" he asked.

"We have a perfect cover," Indy said. "My dad. I'll tell him I met you in the corridor, and we became friends. That'll tickle him. He likes me to have another kid to hang out with. That way he doesn't have me in his hair."

"He doesn't like you?" asked Ivan, arching his brows.

"Oh, he likes me okay," Indy said. "But he likes his work even more. Anyway, we say you live in a distant part of Russia. And the relative who was supposed to meet you at the station wired at the last minute that he couldn't. We ask if you can take a taxi with us to our hotel. You want to find a phone there to contact a friend of your family."

Ivan nodded. "I see. The police won't be looking for me with a party of Americans." Then his face clouded. "But won't your father wonder why I have no baggage?"

"Don't worry," Indy assured him. "My dad is not what you'd call observant. Not about anything less than five hundred years old."

An hour later Professor Jones lived up to Indy's description. The professor barely glanced up from his book when Indy introduced Ivan. Indy asked if Ivan could share their taxi. His dad barely took the time to grunt "okay" before returning to his reading.

When they got off the train in the crowded station, Indy had to look at his watch twice. What Ivan had said was true. It was eleven at night, yet the city was still bathed in daylight. Their taxi took them along the bank of a river that sparkled silver in that light.

"That's the River Neva," said Ivan. "It divides the city."

"Who's that big guy?" Indy asked as they passed a huge bronze statue of a man on a rearing horse.

"He is big," Ivan agreed. "In real life he was nearly seven feet tall. That's Peter the Great. The czar who built this city more than two hundred years ago. He had to drain marshland and dig canals to do it. But he wanted his capital to be on the Baltic Sea, facing Europe. That was Peter's way of turning Russia toward future progress."

"It seems to have done the trick," said Indy. "Russia looks real up-to-date."

"St. Petersburg is," Ivan said. "But Russia is very big. And much of it is far, far from modern."

"I see you know your history, young man," Professor Jones commented. "I hope you listen to him, Junior, and learn something."

Indy decided not to argue with his dad about being called Junior. He had something better to say.

"Maybe I can take a walk around the city with Ivan," he suggested. "I can pick up some history that way."

"An excellent idea," Professor Jones said. "If Ivan doesn't mind, that is."

Ivan flashed Indy a quick, inquiring look. Then he said, "I don't mind at all. It would be fun. The friend of my family does not live far from your hotel. After I call him, it will be easy to walk to his house."

They reached the Hotel Astoria. It was elegant. Again the rich Georgian was paying the professor's bill. As the professor checked in at the front desk, Indy explained his plan to Ivan. "I figured if I walked out of the hotel with you, there'd be less chance of the secret police spotting you. After all, what would an American kid be doing with a Russian rebel? Besides, I'd like to take in St. Petersburg. It looks like quite a place."

"Good thinking. Thanks," Ivan said. "I'll give you a quick tour of the city. I don't want to take a taxi. Too many drivers are informers. And I can't walk straight to my safe house. I have to go roundabout, to make sure nobody is following me."

As Indy was about to leave the hotel with Ivan, Professor Jones made a suggestion. "Perhaps you should take notes, Junior."

"Sure, Dad, sure," Indy said.

But what Indy noted as they walked toward the river was two men behind them.

"Don't look now, but—" Indy said.

"I see them too," Ivan said.

"Maybe they aren't tailing us," said Indy.

"It's easy to find out," said Ivan.

Ivan made a detour that took them past the Winter Palace of the czar. The boys paused in the vast square in front of that immense building. It was covered with gold and seemed to glow in the light.

"Less than ten years ago, in 1905, this square was filled with people from all over Russia," Ivan said. "They had come in peace to ask the czar for reforms in government. They called the czar their 'Little Father.' Their 'Little Father' let Cossack soldiers loose on them. They were massacred."

There was a note of special bitterness in Ivan's voice. But before Indy could ask him about it, Ivan spoke. "They're still behind us," he said. "We have to lose them. I must not lead them to my friends." Then he smiled wryly. "There is another place we must avoid going too. The Peter-and-Paul Fortress. Where the secret police do their torture."

Walking quickly, he led Indy onto a broad avenue. It was lined with glittering stores, ornate mansions, huge official buildings.

"Nevsky Prospekt. The most beautiful street in St. Petersburg and all of Russia," said Ivan. Meanwhile, he hunted for an escape route.

"We'll try this way," he said. He led Indy onto a narrow side street.

"It looks like a maze back there," said Indy. "We can shake them easily."

"I hope so," said Ivan.

The way Ivan was looking about made Indy uneasy. "Hey, you do know your way around here, right?"

Ivan didn't say anything. But the answer was obvious. They turned onto another street and followed it—to a dead end. Indy could see that Ivan was as lost as he was.

"Come on," Indy urged. "Let's get out of this trap while we still can."

But by the time they made it back to the corner, the two men were coming up the street and had spotted them.

Without a word, Indy and Ivan knew what they had to do. They ran for it—as fast as they could. Making sharp turns down nar-

row, deserted, late-night—but still bright—
streets.

Feet kept pounding behind them. And kept
getting closer.

As they turned down yet another street,
Indy gasped. "Hide in that doorway, Ivan.
I'll lead them on a wild-goose chase. By the
time they catch me, you can make your get-
away."

"Thanks" was all Ivan had time to say. He
quickly hid himself.

Indy poked his head around the corner to
make sure the two men spotted him. Then
he took off.

It worked. Both men tore after him. Down
one street, then another.

Better yet, Indy was getting clean away.
There was just one man behind him now.

The other guy dropped out, Indy thought
triumphantly. Then he looked ahead. Uh-oh.

One of the men was waiting for Indy there.
He must have circled the block. The other
man was still on Indy's tail. They were like
two jaws of a trap snapping shut.

Indy wasn't worried, though. He knew exactly what to do. He stopped and waited for the men to reach him from each side. Indy pointed to himself and confidently spoke the magic word: "Americanski."

Indy looked into the face of one, then the other. Both were swarthy, with thick black beards. And neither seemed at all enchanted by the magic word.

In fact, their faces grew even darker as one grabbed Indy by the right arm, the other by the left.

Each wore a look and had a grip that told Indy they wanted to tear him apart.

Chapter 5

The two men started dragging Indy away.
Where were they taking him? Indy remem-
bered what Ivan had said about the Peter-
and-Paul Fortress. He recalled the word *torture*. He decided not to make it part of his
city tour.

He couldn't fight them. They were too
strong. He'd have to go the other way.
Weakness would have to be his strength.

He let himself go totally limp.

The two men looked at the boy. Had the kid fainted? They laid him down on the pavement to examine him.

That was all the breathing room Indy needed. The moment their hands let go of him, he was on his feet and running.

The men were behind him—and gaining. Still worse, in front of him the street came to a sudden end.

He had reached the edge of a canal.

He didn't pause. His dive was perfect. He went into the water like a knife. He stayed under water as long as his lungs held out. When he surfaced, he found he had reached a bridge. It was good to see people crossing the bridge. He swam to the canal bank and hoisted himself out. He saw then he had reached Nevsky Prospekt.

Indy stopped panting long enough to heave a sigh of relief. The two goons wouldn't attack an American on a crowded street. He was safe. All he had to worry about was his soaked clothes. How was he going to explain them to his dad?

It turned out he didn't have to worry. The clerk at the hotel told the dripping kid that he had a separate room. And that his dad had left a request not to be disturbed when Indy returned.

The next morning at breakfast, Ivan's dad said, "I'm glad to see you're wearing a fresh set of clothes, Junior. We see Mr. Kipiani today. We must make a good impression. His funding is vital for my work."

"I thought it would be a good idea," said Indy modestly.

"I hope you had an instructive tour with the Russian boy, whatever his name was," said Professor Jones.

"Very educational," Indy assured him.

"Did you happen to see a street called Nevsky Prospekt?" asked his dad. "That's where Mr. Kipiani lives."

"I know it well," said Indy. "It's in easy walking distance."

After breakfast, Indy strolled with his dad to the mansion of Fedor Kipiani.

A butler in formal dress answered the door

chimes. He led them into an elegant draw-ing room. Kipiani rose from an antique French chair to greet them.

Kipiani was short, neatly built, and nat-tily dressed. He wore a trim European-style goatee and a suit made in London. But un-derneath it all, Kipiani was a Georgian through and through. He loved Georgia. He had made that clear in his letters. And he made it clear now.

"It is important that we investigate all of Georgian history," he told Professor Jones. "The Russian government wants to make us forget our past. It wants us to think we are Russians, not Georgians. It wants us to live a lie. That is why I want you to find and write the truth, Professor."

"With your generous help, I shall," Professor Jones promised him.

"Excellent," said Kipiani. "We will obtain your government travel papers today. We'll leave for Georgia on my private railway car tomorrow."

"The papers today?" said Professor Jones,

raising his eyebrows. "I've always heard that Russian officials are slow."

"They are also underpaid," said Kipiani with a smile. "It is amazing how little money is needed to speed them up a lot."

Kipiani did not say how much he had spent. But it had clearly been enough. By the end of the day, Professor Jones and Indy had been to five different government offices. They had received five different sets of papers without delay. All Professor Jones had to do was ask to see the official in charge of each office and mention Kipiani's name.

The next morning they were on the station platform with Kipiani. "I must say," Professor Jones told his patron. "You got good value for your money."

"We Georgians always get good value for our money," said Kipiani. "We are famous for being good merchants."

"You must be real good," said Indy. "That's quite a railway car you have."

He looked admiringly at the sleek, modern car being hooked up to the train.

Kipiani was looking at his watch. His forehead furrowed. Then he relaxed. A woman approached, followed by two servants.

Indy couldn't tell much about her. Though the day was warm, she wore a cotton coat and a hat with a veil that came over her face.

"This is Miss Tamara Rustavi. She is the daughter of friends of mine," Kipiani said. "She will be traveling with us." Then he looked at his watch again and said briskly, "Let us board. It is so hot out in the sun. I will make the introductions inside."

The inside of Kipiani's railway car made the Nord Express seem shabby. But Indy barely noticed the furnishings. The girl, Tamara, had lifted her veil. And for the first time Indy saw her face.

But it wasn't the *first* time. He had seen that face before.

Ivan's face.

Their eyes met. Indy caught a warning look.

He glanced at his dad. No problem there. His dad, being his dad, noticed nothing.

Very clever, Indy thought. Ivan had dressed like a girl. A perfect disguise.

Then the hat came off. Long brown hair tumbled down. The coat came off, to reveal a white summer dress.

Ivan was not pretending to be a girl. Ivan *was* a girl.

"Tamara has returned from studying abroad," Kipiani said. "Her parents asked me to take her back to them in Georgia when I went. As you see, she is still quite young—not even sixteen. And she is shy about traveling in public among strangers."

Indy opened his mouth—but again he caught a warning look.

He shut his mouth and waited.

He had to wait until the train was well under way. The girl asked him if he wanted to play a game of cards. She indicated a table at the far end of the car.

Kipiani shot her a sharp glance. "Please," the girl said. "I want to practice the English

I have been studying. Otherwise I will start to forget it."

"And maybe I can learn a few words of Russian," said Indy.

"You mean Georgian," Kipiani said sharply. "That is Tamara's native tongue."

"Right. Georgian," Indy corrected himself.

Kipiani could find no reason to refuse the girl's request. He could only nod curtly. Indy and the girl went to play cards at the far end of the car. Indy felt Kipiani's eyes on them all the time.

The girl dealt the cards. Indy spoke to her in a low voice, his lips barely moving.

"There's a game I used to play in school," he said. "It was called show and tell. Want to try it?"

Chapter 6

"I shouldn't tell you, but I want to," Tamara said, still dealing the cards. Her lips, too, barely moved. Her voice was low enough to reach Indy's ears only.

"You can trust me," Indy said.

"I know I can," Tamara said. "And you did save me last night. The very least I owe you is the truth about me."

"Right," Indy agreed.

He picked up his cards and Tamara picked

up hers. They pretended to play. Aimlessly they threw down cards and scooped them up. They were playing a game without rules.

"Besides, I do so want to talk to someone my own age. Or almost my own age," Tamara said. "It has been so long since I've had anyone to talk to. I mean, really talk to."

"You can talk to me," Indy assured her. He looked at her across the table. At her lustrous brown hair, her brown eyes, her flawless skin, her face that seemed to come out of a picture book. He did a quick mental calculation. Tamara was right. They *were* almost the same age. After all, when Tamara was thirty-two, he'd be over thirty. Practically no gap between them at all.

He saw Tamara's lips tighten. She had come to a decision.

"I *will* tell you," she said. "To start with, my name is not Tamara. It is Tamar."

"Oh?" Indy said, puzzled.

"A small difference, you think," Tamar said. "But for a Georgian, very important.

Tamara is a Russian name. Tamar was the name of the greatest of Georgian rulers. Tamar, the warrior queen, who led our nation to power and glory seven hundred years ago."

Indy nodded. It was beginning to make sense. Tamar was not a Russian revolutionary. She was a Georgian revolutionary. That meant Kipiani was one as well. They were probably all part of the same network.

"Your parents named you after her," Indy said, to show he understood. "They're Georgian patriots, and you're one too."

"I am a patriot," Tamar said. "But I am more than just that. I am a—" She paused. Then she managed to say it. "I am a princess."

Now that she had said it, she relaxed. Her explanation flowed more smoothly. "I belong to the Georgian royal family. I am a direct descendant of Queen Tamar."

"Then your parents are the king and queen," Indy said.

Tamar bit her lip. Then she steadied herself. "They *were*—in secret, of course. The czar would not have treated them like fellow monarchs. But they are gone now. They led a group of Georgians who joined the protest in St. Petersburg in 1905. They were among the victims of the massacre."

"And that left you—" Indy began. "But do you have brothers or sisters?"

Tamar shook her head. "I am the only living member of the Georgian royal line."

"That would make you more than a princess. It would make you a queen," said Indy. He felt something close to awe.

"It *will* make me a queen," Tamar said. "In a few months when I am sixteen. And when we mark the seven-hundredth anniversary of Queen Tamar's death. I will be crowned then."

"You worked that out pretty neatly," Indy said.

"*I* did not work it out," Tamar said. "Kipiani did. He has planned it as he has planned everything. He took charge of me after my parents died. He has trained me to be queen ever since. It was he who sent me to Switzerland to get the education that the future queen of Georgia will need after the revolution that will throw the Russians out. The revolution that needs a royal ruler to rally around if it is to succeed."

"You don't sound like you're so happy about the idea," Indy commented.

Tamar looked away from him. She stared at her cards and said, "That is because I am young and weak and foolish. I know I must do my duty. I must be queen of Georgia, as Kipiani says."

She sighed. "But sometimes it is so hard. And so lonely. There is no time or place for play. And no time or place for friends. Even in Switzerland, I did not go to a school with others. I had private tutors. One of them must have been an informer to the czar. Fortunately, Kipiani also has paid informers in the Russian government. He was able to arrange for me to flee just in time. But then somebody else must have tipped off the Russians that I was sneaking back in."

"Spies and counterspies, huh?" said Indy. "Sounds like quite a game. Lucky thing Kipiani is so good at it."

"Yes," Tamar said. "He has shielded his role under cover after cover of deception. So the game goes on and on and on. Sometimes I think it will never end."

At that moment, Tamar's face looked very tired. And very young. Looking at her, Indy actually felt older than she was. And stronger. And he wanted very much to protect her.

"Look, Kipiani is getting suspicious of the game *we*'re playing," he said. He glanced toward the other end of the car. Kipiani was pretending to read a newspaper. But his eyes were fixed on them. "Maybe we should cut off the conversation now. We'll have time to talk later. My dad will be in Georgia for a while."

"Don't count on it," said Tamar. "You don't know Kipiani as I do."

The next day Indy saw what Tamar was talking about. The train pulled into Tiflis, the capital of Georgia.

Indy left the railroad car with the others. He blinked in the dazzling hot sunshine. In the distance he saw high mountains. And beside the station he saw two cars waiting for them.

Kipiani informed them that one car was for Professor Jones, Indy, and himself. The other was for Tamar.

"Your parents are waiting eagerly for you, Tamara," he told her. "You must not delay rejoining them. I suggest you say good-bye to Professor Jones and his son now. Your parents are planning a trip with you. A long trip. I do not think you will be seeing our American guests again."

Indy tried to catch Tamar's gaze, but she refused to look at him.

She gave Indy's dad a polite smile and shook hands with him.

"It was very nice meeting you, Professor Jones," she said. "I wish you the best of luck in your investigation."

Then she did the same with Indy.

"It was very pleasant meeting you," she said. "And best of luck to you, too."

Indy barely heard her. He was far more interested in the touch of her hand. And the piece of paper she passed to him with her handshake.

"Thanks," he said. As he spoke he palmed the piece of paper, then stuck it in his pocket. "Hope to see you again."

Her eyes met his.

"I hope so," she said. "Again, I wish you luck."

Chapter 7

It looked as if Indy was out of luck. As soon as he was by himself, he pulled out the piece of paper Tamar had given him. He was sure she had scribbled down where she was going.

But there wasn't a word on the paper— only a strange sign:

Indy didn't have a clue what it meant. Or where Tamar was now.

But he did know how lonely she must feel. And how much he wanted her to be less lonely.

This wasn't anything mushy, Indy told himself. No way. It was just that Tamar needed help. Help from a friend. Him.

But no luck. Tamar had disappeared. And Indy was left with a month or so to kill in Georgia. And with more than a month's worth of deadly reading in American history.

The next day, when his dad offered him a break from his books, he jumped at it.

His dad was going to visit an ancient monastery up in the mountains. It had a library with manuscripts from the time of the Crusades and even before. Georgia had a long, long history.

Kipiani used his car for the trip. He insisted on going with the professor, to make sure the monks let him see what he wanted.

"I'm afraid it will be dull for the boy,

though," Kipiani said. "Just some old buildings in the middle of nowhere."

"Dull? How could it be dull? It is part of history," Professor Jones said.

Indy thought about a bunch of old buildings in the middle of nowhere. It wasn't very exciting. Then he thought about the book he was reading. On President Millard Fillmore.

"I'd really like to go," he declared.

As the car left Tiflis, Indy began to see that the trip wouldn't be so bad. The road wound through mountains that grew higher and higher. Thick green forests covered the slopes. Snow gleamed on the highest peaks. The country was wild and beautiful.

"These are the Caucasus Mountains," said Kipiani. "And this is the Georgian military highway. It was built hundreds of years ago to supply our frontiers to the south."

Two hours later, they reached the monastery.

"Looks more like a fort," Indy observed. It was surrounded by high stone walls, complete with battlements. And it stood like a fort on a crag overlooking a blue lake.

"There have been times when our monasteries served as forts," said Kipiani. "Times of trouble with foreign invaders. Turks and Mongols and Persians. And finally Russians."

Indy and his dad went with Kipiani and his chauffeur to the huge wooden door of the monastery. Kipiani pulled a chain. A deep bell sounded. A monk with a long beard and a brown robe answered.

He knew who Kipiani was. He bowed slightly to show his respect. Kipiani bowed in return. Then he explained why they were there. The monk ushered them into one of the old stone buildings within the walls.

Indy's dad sat down at a long table lit by an oil lamp. He rubbed his hands together in anticipation as the monk brought him a pile of dusty manuscripts.

Indy sighed. His dad was settling in for a long session.

"If nobody minds, I think I'll take a look around," Indy said.

"I will go with you," Kipiani said instantly.

"Don't bother," said Indy. "Don't worry. I'll show the proper respect to everything here. I just want to get a look at it. I like exploring things on my own."

"I'm afraid I must insist," Kipiani said firmly. "The monks here are most suspicious of strangers. And they speak only Georgian."

"Do as Mr. Kipiani says," Indy's dad said, without looking up from his reading. "He is our host."

That ended the discussion. Kipiani kept close to Indy. They left the library and walked across a cobblestone courtyard.

"There don't seem to be many monks around," said Indy.

"Unfortunately, there aren't many left," Kipiani said. "The czar wants to promote the Russian Orthodox Church. He has cut off almost all funds for the Georgian Church."

"So Georgia has a separate church, too," said Indy.

"We have a separate *everything*," Kipiani said. The passion in his voice made Indy even more sorry for Tamar. Kipiani was a guy who would use anyone and do anything to shake off Russian rule. And Tamar was a puppet in his hands.

They had reached a church. It looked even older than the other buildings here.

"Can I go inside and look around?" Indy asked.

Kipiani hesitated. Then he said, "Let me go first and see. I want to make sure you do not disturb any monks at prayer."

A minute later he was back. "Please enter," he said. "I will show you some interesting things."

The inside was surprisingly well lit. Countless candles flamed in niches in the walls. Daylight sliced in through slitlike openings.

"Observe these paintings," Kipiani said. "Some are truly excellent."

Paintings lined walls and hung on columns. Their colors were bright and strong—reds and blues, purples and golds. Indy walked around the church, looking at them. Some had figures easy to identify, with solid circles around their heads. They had to be saints. But other figures were more difficult. They held mean-looking swords in their hands.

"Who are they?" Indy asked.

"The kings of Georgia," Kipiani said.

"And this one?" Indy asked, pausing before the largest painting of all. It was of a woman in armor. She held a shield in one hand and an upraised sword in the other.

"Queen Tamar," said Kipiani. There was reverence in his voice.

"Tamar?" asked Indy innocently. "Does that name have anything to do with the girl who traveled with us? Tamara, wasn't it?"

Kipiani's voice was curt. "None at all. Tamara is a very common Russian name."

Suddenly Indy froze. Except for his heart, which pounded faster. His eyes had wandered from the painting to the bare stone wall beside it. Carved in the stone was a symbol:

Indy kept his voice casual. "What's that strange-looking sign?"

"The Georgian cross," Kipiani said. "The symbol of our church."

"A cross?" said Indy, puzzled.

"Georgians have grown grapes for wine for thousands of years," Kipiani explained. "The early Georgian Christians made their crosses from the curving branches of their vines."

"Ahh, that explains it," Indy said.

He did not say out loud what it explained. It explained the mark Tamar had made on the piece of paper. And why Kipiani was sticking so close to him now.

Tamar was here, in the monastery. Indy was sure of it. He could practically feel it.

"Time to get back to your father," Kipiani said.

Tamar was so near now. But soon she would be so far away.

Unless Indy thought of something. And the sooner, the better.

Chapter 8

Indy was still thinking hard when he returned to the monastery library. Spotting the Georgian cross had been a stroke of luck. But now he had to make his own luck.

Today, though, was his lucky day.

"These manuscripts are fascinating," his dad declared. "They offer a splendid lead to activities of the Crusaders in Armenia, before they arrived in Georgia. I will have to visit a library in Yerevan, the Armenian capital."

"Armenia?" said Indy. "Where's that?"

"A little to the south," his dad said. "It's not one country now, though. It's split between Turkey and Russia. Yerevan is in the Russian part. It's an easy trip from here."

Meanwhile, Kipiani's face had darkened. "Armenia? Your work is in Georgian history."

"My work is wherever my research leads," said Professor Jones. His voice had a hard edge. One thing about his dad, Indy thought. When it came to scholarship, he wouldn't kowtow to anyone.

Kipiani could see that. He shrugged. "All right. Just so you return to Georgia."

"I will, as soon as I can. Although I can't say when that will be," Indy's dad said.

Kipiani's eyes gleamed craftily. "You should leave your boy behind. He will be made comfortable in my house. And you will not have to worry about him."

Indy had a feeling that Kipiani wanted him as a kind of hostage. To make sure his dad did return.

His dad was more than willing to go along. "An excellent idea. But I hope Junior will not be a bother to you."

"Not at all," Kipiani said. "Actually, I will not be around. I must return on business to St. Petersburg. But my servants will tend to your son's every need."

That was how Indy found himself alone in Kipiani's Tiflis mansion two days later. His dad and Kipiani both were pursuing their plans. Indy was free to pursue his.

His first step was to leave the house early in the morning. He walked through the town. He passed wooden houses painted pale blue and pink and green, with elaborate carvings on their balconies and doorways.

Indy reached his destination. A horse stable he had spied from Kipiani's car.

He was ready to bargain in sign language. But the horse dealer knew English.

"I have been studying your language," he told Indy. "I plan to go to America. My brother is already there. In Fresno, California. Many Armenians are there."

"You're an Armenian?" Indy said.

"Petor Sourian, at your service," the man said. "There are many Armenians here in Georgia. And between you and me, you are lucky to have come to one to rent a horse. The Georgians are not to be trusted so much." Then he smiled. His white teeth flashed under his large black mustache. "Of course, the Georgians say the same thing about Armenians."

"A friendly rivalry, huh?" Indy said.

"Sometimes not so friendly," the horse dealer said. Then he shrugged. "But still, we get on with each other. Anyway, I will give you a better horse than any Georgian. And a better bargain."

The mount was a good one, a magnificent roan. And the dealer refused to take a deposit, even though Indy was ready to part with his tiny bit of cash.

"You are an American," Sourian said. "I trust you. Keep the horse as many days as you want. And pay me by the day at the end."

Sourian stood by the entrance to his stable

as Indy rode away. "Enjoy your ride. The scenery is beautiful. Though you must go to Armenia someday if you want to see real beauty."

But Indy wasn't interested in the scenery. He was interested in getting to the monastery as soon as possible. He had to be careful not to push his horse too hard. He knew that it was both cruel and dangerous to force a mount beyond its limits.

Three hours later, the walls of the monastery came into sight. Indy knew there was no point in trying to enter through the gate. Even if the monks let him in, they'd watch him every minute.

He found a stream and let his horse drink. Then he tethered it in the shade of a pine forest.

He was ready to face his next hurdle. He had his bullwhip in his hand.

All winter long Indy had practiced with his bullwhip. In private. After school on weekdays. Early in the morning on weekends. His skill with it had grown. He had also learned how many things he could do with it.

Now was the time to put into action everything he had learned.

He sent its long lash curling around a battlement on top of the wall. He gave it a tug. It held firm.

"Here we go. Up and over," Indy said. He started hauling himself up to the top of the wall. Crouching low, he looked at the courtyard on the other side. His luck still held. Not a monk in sight.

He lowered himself down to the courtyard. Then, with a flick of his wrist, he shook the lash free. Sticking the bullwhip in his belt, he headed into the church.

More luck. It was deserted. But now what?

He had only the Georgian cross to go by. He went to the wall where it was carved. He knocked on it. Once. Twice. Three times.

He was hoping the wall was hollow. It wasn't. He was hoping for some kind of response. There was none.

Rats, he thought. Back to square one.

He was turning away when he felt something slap across his cheek. Something slithery.

He felt his stomach drop right into his shoes.

He could think of only one thing.

Indy wasn't afraid of much. But he was afraid of one thing very much. More than just afraid. Just the idea of it turned his blood to water, made his mind swim.

"Oh no, not that," he groaned to himself. *"Not a snake!"*

Chapter 9

Gathering all his strength, Indy forced himself to look.

Dangling in front of his eyes was the end of a rope ladder. He looked up.

The ladder led to an opening high in the wall. There a stone door had swung open. Tamar was looking down at him with a finger raised to her lips.

Indy didn't have to be told to be quiet. Or what to do now.

Swiftly he went up the ladder. As soon as he was through the doorway, Tamar hauled the ladder up. She closed the door behind them.

They were in a large, well-furnished room, lit by candles. Clearly Tamar was wearing a traditional Georgian dress. She looked like a real princess.

"Welcome to my kingdom," Tamar said. "Unless you want to call it my prison cell."

"You're a prisoner here?" Indy asked.

"I really shouldn't say that," Tamar said. "I guess I'm just annoyed at being cooped up. Usually I have the run of the whole monastery. But your father's visit made everyone a little nervous. I was asked to give the monks a chance to make sure it was safe each time I left my room."

"This is quite a hideout you have here," said Indy. "I wouldn't have spotted it in a million years."

"A lot of old churches have secret rooms," Tamar said. "Country folk used them to hide from roaming foreign invaders." Tamar smiled. "As soon as I heard that knocking on the wall, I was sure it was you . Somehow I knew you'd manage to find me. Like a knight in shining armor."

Indy felt his face turning red. "More like a detective," he said quickly. "I like to work on my skills. I'm going to need them someday. Besides, it was so boring back in Tiflis."

"Boring." Tamar grimaced. "You don't know what boring is. Sometimes I'm so bored here I could scream. But of course I can't. Because that would give me away."

"Look, I have an idea," Indy said. "I've got a horse outside. A big one. Big enough to carry both of us. Want to go for a ride in the forest? You can take an afternoon off from being a princess. In America we call it playing hooky."

"I must say, I'm tempted," Tamar said. Then she gave Indy a big grin. "In fact, I'm convinced." Her brow furrowed. "But how do we get over the wall?"

"Don't worry," said Indy. "I have a way. I'll let it be a surprise."

Indy noted with admiration that once Tamar made up her mind, she didn't waste time. Without another word, she opened the stone door. She let down the ladder again.

"I'll go first," Indy said. "I'll make sure the coast is clear."

He went down the ladder while Tamar waited above. He went through the empty church and stuck his head outside the door.

That was as far as he got.

A strong arm went around his neck.

A big, sweaty hand clamped over his mouth.

He couldn't see who had grabbed him. The man stayed behind Indy as he pushed him back into the church.

Looking upward, Indy saw Tamar feverishly hauling up the rope ladder.

Then the man holding Indy shouted up to her in Russian—not Georgian, which sounded different.

Indy couldn't understand a word. But he could understand the gesture the man made. The man took his hand from Indy's mouth.

A moment later, Indy felt the cold edge of a knife blade at his throat. The man was telling Tamar what would happen if she didn't come down.

Tamar didn't wait to see if the man was bluffing. She lowered the ladder and came down. The knife was removed, and Indy started breathing again.

"Thanks," Indy said to Tamar. They were shoved side by side against a wall. "I owe you one."

"Don't thank me," she said. "I got you into this."

Indy couldn't argue with that. By now he could see who had grabbed him.

Not one man but two.

Two men with bearded, swarthy faces.

Two men whom he had met before. In the day-bright night up north.

"Those guys are the same ones who trailed you in St. Petersburg," said Indy.

Out of the corner his eye he saw Tamar give a short nod.

But they couldn't say more. There was a

gun in one man's hand. The other guy barked a harsh command. Then the first man used the gun to motion for Indy and Tamar to move out.

They left the church and walked across the courtyard. Through an open doorway in one of the buildings, Indy saw monks bound and gagged. The two goons hadn't had to go over the wall. They could leave by the front door. There was no one to stop them.

Indy started to say something to Tamar. But a guttural command from the man with the gun ended the conversation. Indy had to wait to sort things out with Tamar.

A farmer's wagon with a canvas covering over the back was waiting outside the monastery. It was drawn by two large farm horses. Indy's horse was tied behind it. The guys must have found it. They'd decided not to waste this extra bonus by leaving it behind.

Just as they weren't leaving Indy behind.

First they pulled the bullwhip from his belt. Working swiftly and efficiently, they tied Indy's arms together behind his back. Then they tied his legs together. They did the same to Tamar.

They picked up Indy and dropped him into the back of the wagon. Now he couldn't see anything because of the canvas. Tamar was laid down on the rough boards next to him. A minute later, the jouncing of the wagon told Indy that they were under way.

Indy and Tamar couldn't move. But at least they were free to talk.

"I've got a hunch these guys aren't czarist secret police," Indy said.

"Definitely not," Tamar said. "Police don't operate this way. They would have just marched up and seized me. In St. Petersburg I thought they had a reason not to. They wanted me to lead them to the other Georgians. But not here."

"You have any other enemies?" Indy asked.

"I didn't think so," said Tamar. "But it seems I do. They speak with an accent, but I can't quite place it. Wherever they're from, these people certainly don't seem to be friends."

"Yeah, and this is no joy ride they're taking us on," said Indy.

"But who could they be?" Tamar wondered. "Where could they be taking us?"

"I don't think we should wait to find out," Indy said. "It might not be healthy."

"What choice do we have?" Tamar asked.

"Don't worry," Indy said. "I'll get us out of this bind. Trust me."

Chapter 10

"How did you do it?" Tamara asked, wide-eyed.

Indy had freed his hands and was busy untying his feet.

"Easy," Indy said. "I've been practicing using a bullwhip all winter. Not only did I get really good at it, but I also built up a nice arm muscle. When the guy tied a rope around my arms, I made the muscles bulge as big as I could. When I let them relax, the rope was loose enough to slip out of."

By now Indy was completely free. He set

to work freeing Tamar. Indy was an Eagle Scout. The knots were no problem.

"I just wish they hadn't taken my bullwhip," Indy said. "I'd like to do some practice with it on them right now."

Tamar shook her wrists. She rubbed her ankles to get the blood moving.

"First in St. Petersburg, and now here," she said. "I can see you are a real escape artist."

"You haven't seen anything yet," Indy assured her. The admiration in her eyes made him feel warm. It was like basking in the sun.

"I put myself in your hands," she said, smiling. "What do we do next?"

"We wait until it gets dark," Indy said. "Then we untie the horse from behind the wagon, jump on him, and ride away. Even with both of us on him, he'll be a lot faster than the horses that these goons have. Even if they unhitch them from the wagon in time to chase us."

Tamar nodded. "A perfect plan," she said.

It was perfect—almost. Indy had overlooked just one thing. He forgot to let the horse in on it.

As soon as Indy untied him, the horse gave a whinny that filled the night.

"Easy, baby," Indy soothed. But it was too late. The wagon had already come to a halt. Footsteps were pounding toward the rear. A shot exploded in the air. The horse reared and took off before Indy and Tamar could mount it.

"What now?" asked Tamar.

"We switch to plan B," said Indy. "We run for it!"

Indy planned not to run too fast. He didn't want to leave Tamar behind. But he soon saw he didn't have to worry. Tamar ran like the wind.

The trouble was, the guys behind them were no slowpokes. There was no way to lose them on the road. Indy cut into the forest, with Tamar a half step behind.

It was no better. In fact, it was worse. The noise they made dashing through the under-growth gave their position away.

Indy waited for bullets to whiz through the

air. But there were no more shots. Why weren't the guys trying to cut them down? Indy wasn't sticking around to find out.

"Can you go faster?" he gasped to Tamar.

"Yes, but—" she said.

"Come on, then. One big sprint," Indy said. He put his feet into overdrive.

He took one flying step, another, another, another—and his foot went down and down and down.

He had hit empty space. He was falling, falling—

He was yanked back. Tamar had grabbed him by the back of his belt.

"I tried to warn you," she said. "There are deep crevices around here."

Indy looked down in front of him. He gulped hard. He stood on the brink of an abyss, blacker than the forest night.

"Hey, I owe you another one," he said to Tamar.

That was all he got to say. The two goons had arrived. One had a gun. The other had a piece of cloth in his hand. He pressed it over Indy's nose and mouth.

Indy recognized the smell. Chloroform, he thought. Then he stopped thinking.

He plunged into a blackness deeper than the crevice would have been. Now and then the blackness brightened. Dreamlike pictures floated through his mind. It was as if he were outside himself, watching from a long distance.

He saw himself trying to speak. He saw himself being given a bit of food and water. Then the cloth was pressed over his face again. He smelled the chloroform again. And again he dropped into the bottomless blackness.

Again it seemed he was dreaming. He was swimming under water, far, far down. He started rising. The water grew lighter and lighter, from black to deep green to pale green. At last he broke through the surface. He opened his eyes and blinked hard, as if trying to shake water from his lashes.

Dazzling sunlight blazed through the opening of the canvas flap at the back of the wagon. He turned his head. Tamar was lying beside him, tied hand and foot. He realized he was tied up too. Indy wrinkled his nose. An awful smell filled the back of the wagon. But not chloroform. Something else. Then he recognized it. Kerosene.

"Good. You're awake," Tamar said.

"Yeah, I think so," said Indy. "Unless this is all a bad dream."

"I'm afraid not," Tamar said.

"How long have we been on the road?" Indy wondered.

"I don't know," Tamar said. "They chloroformed me, too. Again and again."

"They've stopped putting us under," said Indy. "That means one thing."

"I know," said Tamar. "We must be getting near our destination."

"At least we'll soon find out where we are," said Indy.

"We don't have to wait," Tamar said. "I already know."

"Where are we?" asked Indy.

"Baku" was the answer.

Indy didn't know what the word meant. But one thing was sure. It didn't sound good.

Chapter 11

"Baku?" Indy asked.

"It's a town on the Caspian Sea. To the northeast of Tiflis, and north of Persia," Tamar said. "We've had quite a trip. Almost three hundred kilometers."

Indy did a quick calculation. "About a hundred and eighty miles."

"Over bad roads," said Tamar. "Maybe it was a good thing we were knocked out. The bouncing around must have been terrible."

"Yeah, my body feels like I was in a fifteen-round fight—and lost," said Indy.

"I feel the same way," said Tamar. "I hope it's not a preview of things to come."

"But, tell me—how do you know we're in Baku?" asked Indy.

"Easy," said Tamar, wrinkling her nose. "By the smell."

"The kerosene?" said Indy.

"Baku is the only place in Russia with that smell," Tamar said. "All of Russia's oil is pumped here. And all of her refineries are here."

"But what would they want with you in Baku?" Indy wondered.

"I've been thinking and thinking. I can't find an answer," said Tamar.

"Let's see," said Indy. "We know they're not secret police. Who else would want to grab you? Maybe you have a rival for the Georgian throne."

"That's not it," said Tamar. "The people here aren't Georgian. They're Azerbaijani. I should have known. The two men who captured us spoke Russian with an accent. But I didn't make the connection until now. My Azerbaijanian is rusty. I haven't studied it for a couple of years."

"A-zer-bai—" Indy said, wrestling with the tongue twister.

"Azerbaijani," Tamar said, sounding out the syllables. "Part of their homeland is in Persia, part in Russia. Another conquest of the czars. Another people who want to be free."

"Maybe they want you to help them," Indy said.

"I doubt it," Tamar said. "Georgians and Azerbaijani aren't the best of friends. And the people working for freedom here aren't royalists. Most of them are oil workers who want social change. In fact, they set off the protests that swept Russia in 1905 by staging a big oil strike in Baku."

Indy shook his head. "That leaves us still in the dark."

"At least there's one bright spot," Tamar said. "The Azerbaijani are Islamic. And followers of Islam don't make war on women."

At that moment, their conversation ended. The wagon had come to a halt.

One of the bearded men crawled into the back of the wagon. He untied the prisoners' feet. Indy and Tamar awkwardly got out of the wagon with their hands still tied. The other man was waiting for them with his ever-ready gun.

They were in the enclosed courtyard of a large mansion. The man with the gun motioned for them to enter through a back door.

The mansion was huge. They passed through rooms filled with beautifully crafted European furniture. On the walls were Persian miniatures and oil paintings from the West. Rare Oriental carpets with designs of intertwined flowers and hunting scenes covered the floors.

"One thing is sure," Indy said to Tamar. "The guy who owns this place isn't any oil worker."

"More likely an oil owner," Tamar replied. "When oil was struck here, landholders became instant millionaires."

"And they know how to protect their millions," said Indy. They had passed many servants in the house. All wore Arabic robes. And all had holsters on their hips. Or daggers in their belts. Or both.

Two servants in black fur hats stood with large curved daggers at the ready in front of an elaborately carved door. Indy got a glance at the carving before the door was opened. Endlessly intertwined snakes with open jaws and forked tongues. *Ughh.*

The sight of the man waiting inside didn't make Indy feel any better.

Like his servants, the man was swarthy and had a black beard. But there was much more of him. Three hundred pounds at the very least. It was hard to tell exactly because of his tentlike black robe. Everything about him was dark. Except for the gold and jewels on ten fingers swollen like sausages.

He was seated on a large Oriental pillow. When Tamar and Indy were brought in, he nodded to two tall, powerfully built servants. They bent and hoisted him to his feet.

He looked at Tamar the same way he must have looked at food. Small, piglike eyes gleamed greedily from folds of fat.

He said something to Tamar in Russian, and she replied in the same language.

He shrugged and smiled. "Yes, I know English," he said with a heavy accent. "I do much business in it. Since you want me to speak it for your little friend here, I will do so. I am a fair man. I owe the boy that much for his help."

"Help? What help?" Indy asked.

"Without you, the princess might have given my men the slip in St. Petersburg." The man's voice made it clear that he enjoyed blowing his own horn. "But when they lost both of you in the chase you led them, it was easy to pick up your trail at your hotel. Then follow you to the princess. Then go to Tiflis on the train with Kipiani's railway car. Then learn where the princess went from there.

"The driver of the car that took her to the

monastery was happy to talk," continued the man. "As happy as the secret police who told us that the princess was returning to Russia. And who agreed to let her get through. It is wonderful how happy money can make people feel."

"And it is amazing what some people will do to get it," said Tamar with a sneer. "I am surprised that you, a Muslim, would kidnap a woman just to collect a ransom."

The man's huge bulk shook with silent laughter. His belly quivered like jelly. The folds of his robe rippled like a tent flap in the wind. Finally he paused. He wiped tears of laughter from his eyes.

"My dear princess," he said. "I'm afraid you don't know whom you are dealing with. But I will not keep you and your little friend in the dark."

Indy couldn't stand it anymore. "Look, my name isn't 'little friend.' It's Indiana. Indy, for short."

"And I am Omar. Omar Feraki," the man said.

"I've heard the name somewhere," Tamar

said. She looked puzzled. "I know! You're one of the richest men in Baku."

"Then you have discovered your first mistake," Feraki said, gloating. "I do not need any ransom money. I can buy and sell your backer Kipiani ten times over."

"Then why do you want me?" Tamar asked.

"It is not I who wants you," Feraki said. His voice shifted to a tone as ominous as thunder. "The one who wants you, the one who will get you, is the almighty, the all-giving Ahriman."

Chapter 12

"Ahriman?" said Indy, totally in the dark.

There was a glimmer, though, in Tamar's eyes. "I think I've heard the name. But I can't remember what it means."

"Come with me," Feraki said. "I will refresh your memory."

Feraki led the way out of the room. He moved lightly for a man of such massive bulk. Two servants herded Tamar and Indy behind him.

They reached a cast-iron elevator.

"Built in France and installed by a French engineer," Feraki said with pride. "It is wonderful what money can do."

But the elevator was not very large. Feraki had to go down solo. When it returned, Indy, Tamar, and their guards squeezed aboard.

They descended smoothly to a large room deep underground. It was brightly lit by electricity. But in its center was a square of darkness blacker than night.

What the—? thought Indy, staring at the darkness. It took a moment to see what it was. A huge cube of black rock. But not like any rock he had ever seen before. Light did not glint off it. The opposite was true. It actually seemed to suck in light, so that the air around it was dim as dusk.

"Weird," muttered Indy.

"Ahriman," Feraki intoned, extending his arms and bowing to the stone.

"Some kind of idol?" Indy asked Tamar.

"Impossible," Tamar said. "Islam forbids idols."

Feraki overheard her. His lips curled. "That was your other mistake. You thought that I followed Islam," he said. "My god was worshiped long before Muhammad was born. And will be worshiped long after Islam dies out."

Tamar's face lit up. "Now I remember where I heard of Ahriman," she said. "Ahriman is one of the gods of Zoroastrianism." Then she looked puzzled. "But he isn't the god that the Zoroastrians worship."

Feraki nodded. "You impress me, my dear princess. Not many know such things."

"I was taught about all the religions I might encounter as a ruler," Tamar said. "Part of my training."

"I still don't get it," said Indy.

"Enlighten the boy," Feraki said to Tamar. "I want to see how much you really know."

Tamar's brow furrowed in concentration. "It's an ancient Persian faith," she said. "It still has followers there. In India, too, where they're called Parsees. They believe that history is a struggle between good and evil. Between the god of light, Ormazd, and the god of darkness"—she paused and swallowed—"the god of darkness, Ahriman."

"Ahriman," Feraki echoed. And again he bowed to the black rock.

"You're *not* a Zoroastrian," she said. "You don't worship the god of light, Ormazd. You worship the god of darkness—" She paused with a shiver.

Indy had been following her closely. He finished her thought. "Ahriman."

"Ahriman, the almighty, the all-giving," said Feraki. His words were swollen with reverence.

"But there is no such worship," Tamar protested.

"There is none that any outsider knows," said Feraki. "For thousands of years, only the select few have served Ahriman in his sacred struggle against the accursed Ormazd. And only the select few have reaped Ahriman's rewards." He smiled. "Rewards like the riches that Ahriman gave me, when black gold spouted from my land."

Then Feraki's expression darkened. "But

now all that is threatened. There are those who want to strip me of all I have. The rising of the rabble in Baku a few years ago was a warning. Only Ahriman can protect me in the coming time of trouble. And only if I render Ahriman a service as great as the danger is."

"A service?" asked Tamar.

"I have a hunch that's where you come in," said Indy. He saw the way Feraki was looking at her.

"But first we must see if Ahriman finds my service sufficient," Feraki said.

Feraki took out a black wax candle and a box of matches. He lit the candle and held it in front of the black rock. Then he began to speak in his native language to his god.

"What's he saying?" Indy asked Tamar.

"That I'm a pure young girl of royal blood," Tamar said. "And that you're a foreigner of noble parentage without a blot on your name."

"Guess he's trying to build me up," said Indy. "Go on. What else?"

"He says that together we will deal the

hated enemy Ormazd a terrible blow," said Tamar. "He asks if Ahriman will be satisfied with this service."

Indy's mouth dropped open. He saw the candle flame sway toward the rock and then go out.

Feraki's face broke into a triumphant smile. He turned toward his prisoners. "I have my answer." He nodded with satisfaction. "The moment my agents told me that there was a royal princess in Georgia, I knew I had found what Ahriman would want. It was worth all it cost to track you down. Ahriman will repay me a million times over."

Indy saw that Tamar had gone pale. He felt the same way himself. But he forced himself to speak. "Look, you can't be serious about this. I mean, this is the twentieth century. People don't believe stuff like that anymore. They don't go and—" But he couldn't bring himself to say it.

Feraki did it for him. "I suppose you imagine I am about to do something barbaric now. Like sacrifice you on an altar down here. With a stone knife, perhaps. Or something just as crude."

"Yeah, something like that," Indy admitted.

"Let me assure you, you cannot guess what your fate is to be," Feraki said. "Don't bother even trying. Especially since it would not be worth the trouble. For you are going to find out very, very soon."

Chapter 13

"I wonder where we're going," said Indy.

"And what will happen to us there," said Tamar.

They were free to say anything they wanted. The five men in the back of the truck with them spoke no English. They were all dressed in black Arabic robes and carrying rifles and curved daggers. Through the open canvas flap at the back of the truck, Indy could see a second truck. Feraki was in the front seat beside the driver. Indy had seen other armed men in black robes and fur hats piling into the back.

They had left Baku hours ago. The winding dirt road had grown rougher and rougher as it led into the mountains.

"I guess we've arrived," Indy said. The truck braked to a halt.

The man opposite Indy motioned to him to get out of the truck. Before Indy obeyed, he gave one last look at the bullwhip stuck in the man's belt. Indy's bullwhip. The guy was one of the pair who had snatched Tamar and Indy from the monastery. He had kept the bullwhip as a trophy. Indy had spent the truck ride trying to figure out how to get it back. No luck.

Outside the truck, they were joined by Feraki and the other armed men.

"Just a short walk now," Feraki said. His eyes gleamed with anticipation.

They went along a well-hidden path that branched off from the deserted dirt road. A few minutes later, they stopped before walled buildings that stood against a hillside.

"Looks like a monastery," said Indy.

"But I don't see any cross," said Tamar.

Feraki, standing beside them, chuckled. "I'll give you a clue to what it is," he said. "Look in the sky above it."

Large birds with wide wings lazily wheeled in the darkening blue edged by scarlet sunset in the west.

"I recognize them. I've seen them back in Utah," Indy said. The chill he felt was not that of approaching night.

"What are they?" Tamar asked.

Indy had to force the word out. "Vultures."

There was an icy silence.

Then Tamar said, "I know what this place is."

Feraki said, "I thought you would, my dear princess. Your education seems to have been quite thorough. But do tell the boy. I'm sure he's dying to know." Feraki smiled as he stressed the word *dying*.

"It's a Zoroastrian temple," Tamar said. "They built a few near Baku. In places where fires burned constantly from pools of oil seeping to the surface."

"Fires?" said Indy. "I didn't think they needed that much heat around here."

"Heat?" said Feraki. He was enjoying himself, like a child playing with an ant, making it run to and fro before squashing it. "That's very, very good."

Tamar enlightened Indy. "Fire is sacred to Zoroastrians. In fact, they are often called fire worshipers. Fire is the supreme symbol of the purity and cleansing power of their god Ormazd. They tend an eternal fire in each of their temples."

Indy nodded. "Okay, I understand that. But where do the vultures come in?"

"I will tell you that," said Feraki. He was impatient to get to the best part. "These worshipers of Ormazd believe that nothing impure must defile the fire of their god. When someone dies, the corpse is not burned. It is laid to rest on the temple roof. There vultures devour it."

Indy looked up at the sky. "Those vultures look pretty cocky. I guess they always know where their next meal is coming from."

"This temple has been here for a long, long

time," Feraki said. "Its priests have hidden it well. From the forces of Islam. From the forces of Christianity. But they could not hide it from me. Just as they cannot defend it from the power of Ahriman."

With that final word, Feraki gestured for his men to move forward. One of them banged with his rifle butt on the temple door. A man in a white robe opened it. He stared into a rifle barrel.

"It's no contest," Indy said to Tamar. The black-robed figures swarmed into the temple. Just a few minutes later, one of the men came to the door and gave Feraki the all-clear sign.

"Now at last I will have it," Feraki gloated. "The sacred fire."

"What are you going to do?" asked Indy. "Put it out?"

"Not at all," Feraki said. "Quite the opposite. I am going to feed it."

Then he said, "But enough questions. You will find all your answers inside. All you'll have to do is look into the sacred fire."

A guard with a curved dagger motioned to Indy and Tamar. Feraki led them through the door and through white-walled rooms to the vast chamber that lay at the heart of the temple. In one corner of the room, white-robed priests stood before the guns of Feraki's men. Feraki uttered a sharp command. The men guarding Indy and Tamar herded them to the other side of the room. Alone Feraki approached the fire in the center.

It was easy to see why the temple had been built here. The circular pool of burning oil was at least five feet across. It formed a miniature lake of flames. A knee-high wall of gleaming white tiles surrounded it.

Feraki stood before the flames. His face was tinted red by their glow. The heat beaded his face with glistening sweat. His voice rang out through the room.

"Sounds like he's gloating," Indy said.

"He is," Tamar confirmed. "He's saying that Ormazd is at last defeated. Defeated once and for all. He says that Ormazd will now do Ahriman's bidding. That good will serve evil. That light will be enslaved by darkness. That the sacred fire will destroy two lives. That—" She stopped.

"Go on," Indy said. "What else?"

Tamar bit her lip. "I'd rather not."

"You don't have to," Indy said grimly. "I can guess. He's saying that the fire will claim the lives of a pure girl and an innocent boy. Anything else?"

"The girl is of royal blood and vitally needed by her people," said Tamar. "And the boy is a foreigner who should be protected by the laws of hospitality. That makes the killing supremely sinful. And makes the victory of Ahriman complete."

There was no mistaking the tone of Feraki's voice as he shouted his final words into the flames. Total triumph.

Indy and Tamar looked around the room. Then they looked into each other's eyes.

Nowhere did they find a spark of hope.

Despairingly they stared at the flames of death.

Chapter 14

Suddenly the flames exploded. That was the only word for it. The flames exploded in a gigantic flash of leaping light.

Blindingly bright, the light blazed around Feraki's huge bulk. Feraki vanished in it even as his last ringing words of triumph echoed in the air.

Half-blinded, Indy had to blink his eyes shut. When he opened them again, the flames of the sacred fire had returned to normal.

Feraki lay faceup and motionless on the floor in front of it.

For another long moment, everyone else in the room stayed still as well. Finally one of Feraki's men managed to free himself from shock. He ran to Feraki and bent over him. Then he screamed out a single word.

Indy didn't need Tamar to translate what the word meant.

Feraki was a goner!

The people in the room began to stir. The armed men looked uneasily at one another, wondering what to do. The Zoroastrian priests, their faces lit with reverence, moved unopposed to kneel before the fire.

Then everyone froze again.

The stillness in the air was broken by the sound of wings flapping. Through a large open window a vulture flew into the room. It was the largest vulture Indy had ever seen. It headed straight for Feraki's body.

Tamar turned her eyes away.

"I can't look," she said.

"We can't stay to look," said Indy. "Let's

get out of here while the getting's good. Come on."

Tamar got the message. Together they started racing for the door.

Two armed men stood on either side of it. Indy recognized them. The same two who had given him the chase in St. Petersburg. The same two who had snatched Tamar and him in Georgia. He wished he could stay around long enough to get even with them. But the best he could do was grab back his bullwhip from the one guy's belt. He and Tamar dodged the men's clutching hands and made it out of the room.

The two men came after them. Feraki might be gone, but they were still doing their job. Habits were hard to break.

This *was* getting to be a habit, thought Indy as once again he and Tamar ran for their lives. They dashed out of the temple building and across the courtyard. The two men were coming after them. It was like a dream where the same thing kept happening over and over—running away from these two guys while the pair gained on them with every step.

Suddenly there was a bang. A bullet whizzed past Indy's ear. The guys had changed the script. They were using their guns—and not just to scare. They no longer had to bring back Indy and Tamar alive. It was hard to hit their targets on the run. But they were bound to get off a lucky shot, unless Indy rang in some changes of his own.

Indy's hand went to his bullwhip. I hope that practice made perfect, he silently prayed. Still running, he wheeled around. He sent the whiplash singing through the air.

It curled around the ankle of the gunman in the lead. Indy used every ounce of muscle to give the bullwhip a sharp jerk. The gunman hit the tiles of the courtyard chin first. The man behind tripped over him and went facedown as well. The gun flew from his hand.

"Hey, now I owe you one," said Tamar as she stood beside Indy.

"It's too soon for thanks. We've just bought

a little breathing space," said Indy. He saw the gunmen already trying to get to their feet. Indy turned to Tamar. "Race you to the truck."

They went out through the door and along the twisting path. Night had fallen, but a full moon lit their way. But it lit Tamar and Indy as well. Indy could hear the thumping steps of the gunmen coming after them again.

The dark shape of the truck looked beautiful to Indy. Even better, the crank was still in the motor. "Get in front," he told Tamar.

He gave the crank a vicious turn. Once. Twice. Three times. At last the motor caught and rumbled.

A moment later, Indy was behind the wheel.

"You know how to drive?" said Tamar, amazed.

"I learned last winter," Indy said. "In America, cars are the coming thing. Soon everyone will have one. I figured I'd get a head start."

A head start was what they had now. But not much of one.

Behind them Indy heard the sound of another motor. The gunmen were in the second truck, tearing up the dirt road in hot pursuit.

"Come on, baby, *go!*" Indy muttered. He pressed the accelerator to the floor.

The truck was careening wildly, bouncing like a jumping jack. But their lead was holding.

Tamar was sitting beside Indy and holding on for dear life.

"I've never been on a ride like this," she gasped. "They ought to put some kind of belt on the seats, to strap you in."

"Yeah, maybe they will someday," Indy said. He was concentrating on the hairpin turns. "They could call it a safety belt. We sure could use something right now."

A few moments later, though, he was breathing easier. As they came around one last sharp turn, the road straightened and leveled off. They were out of the hill country. From here on it was a straight run to Baku—and law and order.

"All we have to do is hold our lead," Indy said. "And we're home free."

Then he said, "Ooops."

The truck was bouncing violently once more.

"The road's gotten bad again," said Tamar.

"I hate to say it, but it's not the road," said Indy. "We've got a flat."

"A flat?" said Tamar. "What does that mean?"

"It means we have to get out of this truck and run for it," said Indy. He braked the truck to a skidding stop.

"Maybe we can get out of sight before they get here," Indy said. But by the time he and Tamar were out of the truck, the other truck had screeched to a stop.

"Here we go again," said Indy. "Won't we ever get those guys off our tail?"

"If only the moon would go behind a cloud," panted Tamar, running beside him.

The moon kept shining brightly. Its light bathed the black shapes of oil rigs all around them. They were running through an oil field that was closed for the night.

Indy glanced over his shoulder. He saw a gunman running after them. Just like before.

Then a thought hit him.

There was just one man behind Indy. Just like before, in St. Petersburg.

He knew what was happening. These guys *were* creatures of habit. They were pulling their trick again. One of them was giving chase. The other was circling around to cut off escape. Indy and Tamar were running into a trap.

"Tamar, we have to—" Indy started to say.

But he didn't know what they could do. Then he saw it was too late to do anything.

The other gunman came around an oil rig and stood in their path, his gun leveled.

The one behind them kept coming, his gun leveled too.

Just like before. Except this time the men didn't want to make a capture.

In the moonlight Indy could see their eyes narrow as they stopped, raised their pistols, and took aim.

Chapter 15

It is amazing how fast you think when you face deadly danger. And amazing what you think of.

What popped into Indy's mind as he saw the guns being aimed was a book. *Ten Bullets to Tombstone*, by Sam Magee.

An old gunslinger was giving a green kid advice. He said that when you shot a gun, the barrel kicked upward. So when somebody was taking a shot at you, you should dive low. "Bite the dirt, boy" were the words he used.

"Bite the dirt," Indy shouted to Tamar as he dove low.

It was a good thing her English was excellent. So were her reflexes, and she instantly followed Indy's lead.

At that second, both gunmen fired.

The bullets hummed over Indy and Tamar as they lay facedown on the ground.

Before they could raise their heads, they heard a loud whooshing explosion. Two explosions, really, joined together.

Indy raised his head. He was dazzled by a geyser of fire.

He turned to the opposite direction. Another fireball lit the night.

Both gunmen vanished from sight. Indy and Tamar went to investigate. They saw the gunmen's weapons lying abandoned on the ground.

"The guys took off and ran," Indy said. "I guess the flames made them kind of nervous, after what they saw in the temple."

The twin fires were starting to burn down. Indy and Tamar were able to see they were two oil storage tanks that had turned into torches.

"The guys' bullets must have hit them," Indy said. "It was like lighting a match to a couple of gas tanks."

There were shouts in the distance. The sound of a pistol shot. And silence.

"Watchmen," said Indy. "They must have collared the thugs. Let's make tracks before they get to us. It would be pretty hard to explain all this and even harder to get anyone to believe it."

The gunmen's truck was parked behind the one that Indy and Tamar had used. Indy started the motor, and they headed down the road toward Baku. But now they couldn't escape coming up with hard explanations for their own tough questions.

"I'll never forget how the flame leapt out to destroy Feraki," Tamar said. "Yet it left his body unmarked. As if it did not want to defile itself. The god of light preserved his purity."

"You don't believe all that stuff, do you?" Indy said. He thought this would be a good time to show Tamar how level-headed he was. Wise beyond his years. Mature.

"It's hard not to believe your own eyes," said Tamar.

"I'd rather look at it scientifically," Indy declared. "If I'm going to be a good archeologist, that's the way I have to see things. I figure this was a freak accident. A bubble of natural gas rose to the surface of the oil pool and exploded. It came and went too fast to burn Feraki. But the shock did him in. A guy that fat had to have a bad heart."

"And the vulture that flew in?" said Tamar.

"He was just impatient," said Indy. "It must have been past his feeding time."

Tamar shook her head in doubt. "There are things that science can't explain. I think you will find that out when you become an archeologist and explore the unknown."

Indy had to nod. "Maybe so. I guess the future will tell."

Tamar smiled. "I don't think that future is very far away. You are learning already."

Then her face clouded. "Speaking of the future, we have to decide what we do now."

"That's one thing I do know," Indy said. "We have to try to get back my horse. A nice guy back in Tiflis trusted me with it."

The sky was turning light as they drove into Baku on a road skirting the sea. The rim of the purple Caspian was already stained pink by the summer's early dawn. They drove past the shacks of workers and the mansions of millionaires, past ancient mosques and new Russian churches. Indy stopped the truck halfway down the block from Feraki's mammoth mansion.

"Let's hope he took most of his manpower with him to the fire temple," Indy said. "His servants looked real mean to mess with."

It seemed that Feraki hadn't taken *most* of his servants with him. He had taken them *all*.

There was no one guarding the entrance to the inner courtyard. No one in the courtyard. No one watching from the windows. There was only the horse, tied to a post. Its saddle and harness lay on the ground nearby.

As Indy had thought, Tamar fit easily behind him. And their combined weights did not bother the big animal. They left the courtyard and trotted down the street.

"Well, back to Tiflis," Indy said.

"Yes, back to Tiflis," Tamar agreed.

"I guess there's some kind of railroad connection we could find," Indy said.

"Yes, I suppose there is," Tamar agreed.

"On the other hand—" Indy said.

"Yes? On the other hand?" Tamar said. Her voice had suddenly perked up.

"I know it might sound crazy," Indy said. "But we could try riding the horse all the way back to Tiflis. I mean, I've had plenty of experience camping out. And we could pick up some food and other stuff on the way. It would take a few days, of course. But I wouldn't mind spending some time in the open. Maybe you've never tried it, but you just might like it."

"Crazy?" Tamar said. "It doesn't sound crazy. It sounds wonderful. Days of freedom. Days and days of freedom. Let's go."

She sounded so eager that Indy felt that

he would have to be the practical one. "It'll work out okay. If I know my dad, he won't be back for a week or so. Kipiani is away. And we can wire the monastery that you're okay. That they shouldn't worry. You'll get back in plenty of time to be crowned queen."

Indy heard Tamar clear her throat behind him. Excitement trembled in her voice. "I want to tell you something nobody else knows. I think you should be the first. I'm not going to be queen."

"What?" Indy said, startled. "Did Kipiani and his followers change their mind?"

"No," said Tamar. "I have changed my mind. Or rather, I've made up my mind. I've made my own choice for the first time in my life."

"You mean you don't want to be a queen?" said Indy. He turned his head to look at Tamar.

Her face was serious. Yet at the same time it was glowing with joy. "I have never really wanted to be queen. I have wanted to live my own life, in my own way. But always I was told it was my duty. That Georgia needed me to gain its freedom. But remember that book you lent me on the train? The book about your revolution?"

"I sure do," said Indy. "I've practically had to memorize it."

"You Americans did not need a king or a queen to win independence," Tamar said. "All you needed was courage and a desire to be free. The Georgians have both. And what they don't need is to throw off the rule of a czar only to have a new royal family over them. I will keep working for Georgia. But for a Georgia that belongs to the future—not the past. Thanks to you. And your book."

"Yeah, books can be real handy sometimes," Indy said. He thought of *Ten Bullets to Tombstone*. He'd have to write Sam Magee a fan letter when he got home.

But right now he had a nice ride ahead of him, with a swell friend. Maybe he'd see some more of her in Tiflis. And after that— who knew?

Historical Notes

St. Petersburg was renamed Petrograd in 1914. In 1917, a revolution that began there overthrew the czar. The government that replaced him was overthrown the next year, when opposing forces stormed the Winter Palace. The Communist Party under its leader, Lenin, then seized supreme power.

During the civil war that followed, the capital of Russia was moved to Moscow, where it remains today. At the same time,

Petrograd was renamed Leningrad. Then Tiflis became Tbilisi.

Poland, Georgia, and Azerbaijan all became independent republics during the Russian Revolution. Poland kept its independence by winning a war against an invading Russian army. During World War II, however, the country was divided between Germany and Russia. Then Poland was conquered entirely by Germany. After Germany's defeat, it fell under powerful Russian influence.

Georgia and Azerbaijan enjoyed even less success in their search for independence. They remained independent for less than three years before they were absorbed into the new Communist Russian empire. It called itself the Union of Soviet Socialist Republics (U.S.S.R.). In the past few years, however, with the slackening of Communist control in Russia, Poland again has achieved almost total independence. At the same time, strong new demands for independence have sounded in both Georgia and Azerbaijan. What the future holds for these independence movements remains a question that only coming events can answer.

Needless to say, Princess Tamar does not appear in the pages of history, since she removed herself from power. It could be said, though, that many years later she and Indiana Jones did meet again and—

But that is another story.

TO FIND OUT MORE, CHECK OUT...

A Day in the U.S.S.R. Published by Collins Publishers, 1987. On May 15, 1987, a hundred of the best photojournalists from over twenty countries were positioned throughout the fifteen republics of the Soviet Union. For twenty-four hours they were free to photograph whatever they wished. The result is this superexciting oversize book that the whole family will enjoy. You'll see people and places from Baku to Siberia, as well as some of the same countryside and buildings Indy saw. Full-color photographs with short captions.

Soviet Union. Text and photographs by Planeta Photographic Service. Published by Mallord Press, 1989. An interesting text weaves together excellent photographs of art, architecture, and people. This big, beautiful book will give you the flavor of all the Soviet republics—past and present. All ages.

"Leningrad, Russia's Window on the West" by Howard LaFay. Published in *National Geographic*, May 1971. A brief history of the city, with the accent on contemporary life. See the palaces and bridges Indy and Tamar saw when Leningrad was St. Petersburg. Maps and color photographs.

Let's Visit the U.S.S.R. by Julian Popescu. Published by Burke Publishing Company Limited in 1967 and revised in 1984. An easy-to-read overview of the fifteen republics of the Soviet

Union. Crops, natural resources, industries, geography, and history. Black-and-white and color photographs, a map, and an index.

Soviet Union...in Pictures (Visual Geography Series) prepared by Stephen C. Feinstein. Published by Lerner Publications Company, 1989. A short survey packed with facts and photographs plus maps and an index. This book and *Let's Visit the U.S.S.R.* are perfect for a social studies report.

Soviet Georgia (Places and Peoples of the World) by Michael and Randi Boyette. Published by Chelsea House, 1989. Everything you'd ever want to know about Georgia, plus some information about Azerbaijan. Helpful outlines of history and facts. Maps, photographs, and an index.

SHARE THE ADVENTURE!

Follow the adventures of Young Indiana Jones through the pages of The Official Lucasfilm Fan Club Magazine. Each issue has exclusive features, behind-the-scene articles and interviews on the people who make the *Indiana Jones* films as well as *Star Wars!* Plus there are special articles on the Disney theme-park spectaculars, Lucasfilm Games as well as Industrial Light & Magic — the special effects wizards! You can also purchase genuine collectors items through the club's official catalog such as theater one-sheets, toys, clothing, as well as products made exclusively for members only!

YOUR MEMBERSHIP INCLUDES:

A fantastic 10th anniversary *Empire Strikes Back* Membership Kit including:
- Exclusive *ESB* One-Sheet (originally created for *ESB,* but never produced!)
- Embroidered Fan Club Jacket Patch!
- Two *ESB* 8x10 full color photos!
- *Star Wars* Lives bumper sticker!
- Welcome letter from George Lucas!
- Full-color Membership Card!

PLUS:
- One-year subscription to the quarterly full-color Lucasfilm Magazine!
- Cast and crew fan mail forwarding!
- Classified section (for sale, wanted & pen pals section!)
- Science Fiction convention listing!
- And more!

JOIN FOR ONLY $9.95